All According to the Divine Plan: Author's Edition

Written by Albert Oon

Art by @An_dres_art

SHORT STORIES WITH EXTRAS

Chapter 1 – Forceful Changes

I'm glad that I managed to get out of work today with no one noticing. There was a project I was supposed to finish but that can wait until tomorrow. Besides, the other guys on the team can handle it. It's not like my input is important. Now that I'm back home, I throw aside my jacket and everything in my pockets on my bed and sit down on the floor and turn on my favorite show while browsing my phone for the next thing I want to spend my paycheck on.

"Hello, Gabriella," a monster-

looking thing says as it comes out of my TV.

Startled by this thing's

appearance, I take out my small personal pistol and shoot at

it three times only for my shot to hit everything behind it.

"What the?" I say not believing that my shots had no effect.

"Don't be so rude. I'm your guardian angel."

"Get out of my house!" I shoot the thing another three times to no effect again.

"Aren't you worried about all your precious possessions?"

"I can always buy more and repair the damage done. If you were my guardian angel, you'd know how much money I have."

"I know of your possessions all too well. They are the reason why God has allowed me to manifest myself today. Soon, a storm will pass by here and take all of it away, so you better get to the basement before you are destroyed with them."

Before I mention that I haven't heard anything about a storm coming through here, the sound of thunder, rain, and heavy winds outside. Even though it looks bad, I'm not worried. I prepared my house for this and my house should be strong enough to endure the brunt of it. Still, I go downstairs and hunker down just in case.

 Uck. I can't believe that thing ruined my night's plans and now I have to worry about paying for damages because of the bad storm. On top of the things that I bought, my bank will have a really bad dent that sets back the future vacations that I have planned this year plus the other stuff I want to buy.

The monster appears in the basement with me. "I'm glad that you took my advice."

"Listen, you, I don't care what you say you are. Just leave me alone-" The sounds of tearing and things being destroyed above me shut me up and make me doubt if my house is really okay, especially since the walls of my basement are beginning to crack. Is the storm really that bad? The storms around here haven't really been known to destroy homes. I'm tempted to go upstairs to check right now, but I wait until the storm calms down before I do and sure enough, my worst fears are realized as I see that my entire house is gone along with most everything in it. Around me is what remains of the house and a few of the things I had. It doesn't matter that they're here since everything is broken beyond repair.

 "It's time to leave this all behind and move into a better life that's been prepared for you."

"A better life?! Who are you to say what's better for me after destroying everything that I had and leaving me in the rain?!"

"You'll see soon enough. Go down the road and a young man, faithful to God, will pick you up in his car. He'll be the one providing for you from now on and be your husband."

"I don't need anyone to do anything for me! I've been taking care of myself for years without anyone's help, so I don't need that boy, you, or God's help."

"So, would you rather stay here in the pouring rain in the wreckage of your old home or find shelter?"

"I still can stay in my basement-"

When I take a look back in my basement, the cracks have given way to mud as all the walls cave in and ruin the last of what I had. Now, I have nothing that I own besides my phone, my pistol, and the clothes on my back.

"Will you take my advice now?"

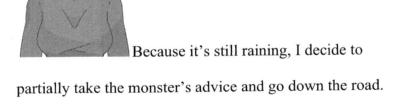

Damn monster. I don't need its help. I don't need anyone's help. It's going to cost me a lot to rebuild since I haven't bothered with home insurance because I wanted to put my money into building it to be stronger and buy more things and go on expensive vacations. I'll have to work overtime and push my plans back even further, but I can get it done without anyone's assistance.

Because it's still raining, I decide to partially take the monster's advice and go down the road.

The closest apartment building is miles away in a different part of the state and will take me a while to get to any place to rest. Cars pass by me every now and then with one driving through a puddle and splashing me with water further drenching me. This is the worst day of my life. I'm both hoping for and dreading someone stopping to help me. If it's the boy that monster talked about, I'll have to turn him down. Sure enough, just like the storm, a car unexpectedly stops on the side of the road without me waving at it and a young man steps out of it.

This boy puts on a smile as he approaches and waves at me. "Excuse me, miss? I can drive you to my house to help you get out of this storm."

"Get lost, kid! I don't need anyone's help, especially from your God. He's taken away my home and everything I had in it through a monster that won't stop following me."

"What are you talking about? Your house and everything in it is destroyed? I'm sorry to hear that. Look, we'll go back to my home, I'll cook us up something, and try to help you out as best I can from there."

"I said get lost!"

"Woah, woah, woah! Calm down! I'm

just trying to help."

"Calm down?! How could I possibly

do that when your God ruined all my plans?! I will not have

him taking any more control of my life and I don't care what I have to do to get him out of it!" I pull the trigger on my pistol only for it to click. Oh, that's right. I never loaded it again after I fired it. Since I'm out of bullets, I try hitting the boy with the pistol, but he takes it from me, throws it away, and then grabs me by the wrists.

 "Get your hands off me!"

 "If you stop trying to hit me I will! Listen, you have three options here; calm down and go

home with me, stay in this storm in the hopes of someone else pulling over to pick you up, or walking hours in the storm to find someplace safe."

"Tch. You have a point. Okay, I'll go to your house."

"Thank you." The boy lets go of my wrists and keeps his hands up as if I'll hit him again before turning around and running to his car with me behind him. "So, what's your name?"

"Shut up! I don't want to talk right now." Deciding to take my advice, the boy nods and keeps his eyes on the road. You'll get your way for now until the storm is over, monster, and then I'm leaving this kid.

"We'll see about that."

"Can you leave me alone for a second?!"

"Who are you talking to?"

"That monster that's been ruining my life! Can't you see it in the car? It was just talking to me!"

"I don't see it and I didn't hear anything."

"God has allowed you to be the only one who can see and hear me. He is also dulling the young man's sense of reason as is beginning to think that he should be dropping you off to authorities to be put in a psych ward, so I'd calm down if I were you."

I'm assuming you can hear my thoughts as well?

"Yes, it's for your convenience so you won't look crazy in public if you want to talk to me."

Ignore it, ignore it! I don't want to acknowledge its existence, so it has less of a reason to talk to me. Thankfully, it says nothing else before we get to the boy's house. It's a small rancher in a neighborhood of small houses. The inside of it is decorated with crosses, what look to be religious statues, and pictures of him with presumably his parents, family, and friends.

"I'll start making soup and tea for us. Feel free to take a snack from the cabinet, drink from the fridge, and turn on the TV. Oh, you can also use the shower and use the clothes I have since you're soaked."

After sneezing, I say, "I'm fine! I don't need anything except for a phone charger." Once I get a phone charger, I plug in my phone since it's dead.

With nothing else to keep me busy, I turn on the TV and watch the news. They admit they didn't know of the storm passing through the area before talking about the daily news. The newscasters talk about where I work at going bankrupt.

"What?! How?!" My question is answered by a guy from where I work saying that they were losing lots of money because of mistakes made by their accounting department and specifically calls out me by my full name and talks about how lazy and incompetent I was. "Bastard! You piece of trash, how dare you say that about me and call me out like that!" Before I know it, I receive an email from the company telling me that I'm fired. Now I'm really screwed with hardly any money, no job, and my name publicly ruined. I also doubt that I'd be able to get a good job in this economy where businesses are more likely to fire employees than hire them.

"Wow, that guy must've hated you with the way he described the way you worked and how he blamed you for the company falling into bankruptcy. Can he even publicly do that?"

"I hope not so that he suffers for it!" I'm sure that monster has had its part to play in this. Admit it!

"Come now. I can't be the reason behind everything. It's true that you were lazy at your job and the mistakes that you made cost it too much in the end."

I didn't think that all the little mistakes I made would add up like this. With all my plans in shatters, I sit on the floor unable to think of what to do next. Wait a second! Hey, monster, fix this! You said there's a better life prepared for me right?

"Correct and your prayer has been answered before you mentioned it. You are currently in your better life. As I have said before, this young man will be providing for you and will be your husband."

Hearing that the boy will be my husband again actually starts to have an effect on me as I finally begin to think about it. Husband?! That boy is going to be my husband?!

He is. Besides God, your hearts were made for one another.

"Dinner is ready. Come and sit at the table with me." The dinner that he's made is irresistible to me because I'm hungry and thirsty. I've managed to eat it all without fully enjoying it or really wanting to eat it. "I'm glad you liked it," the boy says with a satisfied smile on his face.

"Sh-shut up. I'm just hungry is all," I say before sneezing.

"I really think you should-"

"Yes, I know!" Since I'm still feeling cold and drenched, I give in to the boy's request and take a shower. The clothes that I pick out are like the red sweater that I have, but because it's a boy's it looks like I'm wearing a large sweater dress. This feels so ridiculous wearing his clothes.

"I've changed the TV since nothing good is on the news like always. I hope you don't mind."

"I prefer it actually." If I saw that guy's face and hear his voice for a second longer, I would've destroyed the TV. Sitting on a separate chair, I watch TV with the boy while not really paying attention to it. It's really starting to hit me now that everything has completely changed and I have no control over it. Even if I were to do something, it could be instantly ruined as I've been shown today.

Before I know it, the boy hands me a blanket and looks at me with that smile that he always has on his face. "You looked like you were still cold so here's this blanket. Do you need anything else?"

"N-no, I don't. I don't need anything. Also, stop looking at me like that."

"I'm sorry for what happened to you today. You can stay here as long as you like."

He's being so kind to me despite the fact that I'm a stranger and was going to kill him. "Th-thank you. Can you stop smiling at me like that?"

"Like what?" he says before I slap him in the face.

"What did you do that for?"

"For smiling at me the way that you were. Now leave me alone. I'm beyond tired."

"Okay. It's about time I'd get to bed since I have work tomorrow. The couch turns into a bed by the way so you can use that to sleep on rather than just sleeping on the couch itself. If you need anything, don't be afraid to ask. By the way, my name is Connor."

"I know they said it on the news, but my name is Gabriella." Connor says it's nice to meet me and gives me that smile of his one more time. I get up and am about to slap him again, but he leaves the room before I do. As I lay on the couch bed, I feel colder than usual now that he's gone. He is a nice guy. Still…my future husband? Ridiculous. It may not be too outside the realm of possibilities given what's happened today. Everything I had including the control over my life that I thought I had is gone today. Truthfully, I could just go back out into the storm again and defy this life that's being given to me, but who knows what God would do to put me back on his track. Connor would also go out looking for me and I already feel like I wouldn't want to trouble him with that because of how nice he's been.

"Someone is starting to have feelings."

Shut up! I don't know what it is. I'll figure out what I'm going to do tomorrow morning. All I can do right now is sleep hoping that the future will not be as worse as today was and that this so-called better life is actually what it's supposed to be.

Chapter 2 - Coming Around

"Good morning! I made waffles for breakfast."

After stretching, I get up and sit at the table. "Thank you. It tastes good." We finish eating breakfast and Connor cleans and puts the dishes in the dishwasher before taking his coat.

"I'll be going to work now and will be back by five thirty. I've left my phone number on the table so you can call me if anything comes up, okay?"

"Sure." For some reason, I have a feeling within me that doesn't want him to leave, but I wave goodbye as he says goodbye and leaves me alone in his house.

"Don't worry. I'll always be by your side. I have been since you were born after all."

I'd rather you'd not, but I guess I can't do anything about it. With the time I have, I call the contractors and everyone associated with my house to let them know what happened. By the end of it, I agree to pay them to clean up the ruins of my house and they agree to cancel my bills. I guess it's what I get for not getting any insurance for it when I paid for it to be built.

That's all I really had to do today and it's still morning. Connor isn't expecting me to do something so I could poke around to see what he has that I can keep myself busy with. Let's see here. Video games, cartoons, anime, and movies. This is all stuff that a boy his age would be interested in. Why am I getting the feeling that I could take Connor's valuables and sell them to help me settle down somewhere? The temptation from last night is also giving me the idea to kill him when he gets home so that I could have better control of my life and ruin God's plan for me.

"Those are the whispers of demons that I am trying to hold off. Keep yourself occupied so that they don't occupy your mind."

I must admit that you're right for once. I don't need anyone else trying to take control of my life. Hmm. You know what? Connor might think that I'll take advantage of his kindness and be lazy all day. I'll prove him wrong by cleaning the house. It's not much since it's a rancher so I get it done with all the dusting and vacuuming in roughly two hours. There cannot be one speck of dust left so that it looks like I didn't do a lazy job.

 Hmm. I feel better after getting that done. Strangely enough, I feel free and at peace for some reason. Maybe it's because I'm free of the responsibilities over my house and the job I once had. How about I make Connor dinner too? That'll really make him think that I'm not lazy and also worth keeping around. What do you think I should make him?

"His guardian angel tells me that he wants to make pasta for dinner today, so make that."

You can talk to his guardian angel from this far away?

"Amazing, isn't it? I and other angels are pure spirit, which means that I am not limited to one space."

Interesting. Okay, I've made pasta for myself before so it should be easy. Connor should be home in an hour or so. This day has really flown by because of how busy I've been on the phone and cleaning up around here. Anyways, I manage to finish making

dinner and setting the table before he comes in.

"Hello, Gabriella. Oh! You've

made dinner for me. Wow, pasta. I was going to make that

today. Thank you!"

"I've also cleaned the house too.

You don't really get around to doing it, do you?"

"Heh. I try to clean it every two weeks, but it usually ends up being every three weeks because I forget or am too tired to bother with it. Thanks for that too." Connor sits down and we enjoy dinner together. During this, I explain the situation with my house to which he says that he still doesn't mind having me stay here, especially after everything I've done today.

"Are, um, are you okay?"

"I'm fine. Why?"

"You seem different and happy. I like seeing that smile on your face rather than the scowl that you usually have."

"…smile? I don't know what you're talking about, and what do you mean that I usually have a scowl on my face?"

"Agh. Why did he have to mention it? I enjoyed seeing you happy for once. It's true that you've been smiling all day and that you usually do have a scowl on your face."

"It's…nothing. Forget I said anything. Anyways, I'll be off work for the next couple of days and the weekend. Is there anything you wanted to do together?"

"Why do you have off Thursday and Friday?"

"I just wanted to use the paid time off I've been accumulating. I have a lot of it and I thought I'd use it so I told my boss last week that I'd be taking a couple of days off and he said it was a good thing because I rarely use it other than during the holidays and summer."

"Okay, I guess. Um. We'll talk about it tomorrow. I don't know what I want to do yet." Connor agrees to make a decision tomorrow and for the rest of the night, we sit together on the couch and watch TV. For a while, it doesn't hit me that we are sitting next to each other.

"Hm? Is something the matter?"

"Huh? No. Is something the matter with you?"

Connor casually preemptively covers his face with one hand as if I'm going to slap him for smiling. "No. You seem tired. Worked a little too hard today, didn't you?"

"N…no, I haven't…"

"Okay-Gabriella-!"

Drowsiness overtakes me and I fall asleep in an instant. This is strange. I feel more comfortable and at peace than I have in years. There's a warmth in my arms that's the source of it. It beats like a heart and its beats feel like it beats with my heart as if the two were singing together. An invisible force feels like it's trying to push me away from it, but I hold on as tightly as I can to it until I wake up and see that I'm holding onto Connor with both of my arms and my head resting on his shoulder.

 I slap him. "Hey, what were you doing letting me sleep on you?!"

 "You passed out on me, it's not my fault! I tried to wake you up and get you off me but you kept clinging to me, so I just left you to sleep on me for the hour."

Connor then gets up, says it's about time that he goes to bed, and leaves. Part of me wants him to stay with me so I can sleep on his arm again...

No, no, no! It's too embarrassing to think about. For tomorrow, I think about making breakfast for Connor, so I set the alarm on my phone and wake up early in the morning around eight o'clock. He's also up as well and is getting stuff out from the fridge and cabinets.

"Good morning, Gabriella. For breakfast, I was thinking about making-"

"No, no, I'll be making breakfast. It's why I put the alarm on my phone," I say while leaping off the couch and butting into the kitchen. "I'll be making…" What does he want?

"A bagel, egg, and cheese sandwich."

"Bagel, egg, and cheese sandwiches."

"I'll get everything for that out and help you make it. You don't need to-"

"No, no, no. You don't need to do anything. Go sit down. You shouldn't be doing anything on your day off."

"Cooking isn't much trouble. Plus, I like doing it."

I pick up a knife and point it at Connor. "I said sit down. Now."

"Alright, alright. I get your point now."

"You better…I might just stab you because you said a knife joke."

"I'm sorry. Why do you make breakfast so badly?"

"Because if I'm staying here while you go out and work, I have to do something rather than just being lazy."

"I appreciate what you're doing, but you don't have to do anything for me. I'm not going to kick you out-"

"Ah! No more arguing. You can set the table if you want and put something on TV."

Connor reluctantly agrees with me and does what I said.

After eating breakfast and deciding what to do, we go out to a nearby nature trail that we take a nice walk down. He's been wanting to go out for a walk on the trail and since I have no better idea, I agree with him.

"Haven't you walked through any of these nature trails? Our state is famous for them."

"No, it's never really interested me."

"But you have to admit that it's all beautiful and calming; the fresh air, the tall trees, and beautiful flowers and scenery."

"And all the annoying bugs and creatures in the forest. Uck."

"Where do you work?"

"I work with the local Catholic

diocese and paper with their marketing and coordinating

events and parishes so that everyone is on the same page

and working together." I grunt in response not really

surprised at what his job is. Connor does seem like the kind of person who can convince people to work together. "Can I ask about something you mentioned earlier?"

"Sure, what is it?"

"When we first met, you mentioned my God and a monster that's been ruining your life? You also said that you would didn't care what you had to do to get rid of God's influence in your life when you had your pistol pointed at me."

He's silent as if waiting for me to say something so I say, "Right...what about it?"

"Mind telling me what this monster is and what my part in it is? I've been praying and thinking about it over the past couple of nights. There are a few possible answers in my head, but I want to hear what you say." Hmmm. How do I explain this without him thinking

that I'm crazy?

"Just say what you know. I'll

help you."

Alright, I guess. "The monster claims

to be my guardian angel. He appeared to me and told me

about the incoming storm. After my house was destroyed,

he told me that this is the start of my better life with you

playing the part of my…husband."

 Wait, hold on, why did I say

that last part?!

 "You're welcome."

"Uh, future husband?"

"Y-yeah. I'm sorry. My

'guardian angel' was helping me explain things. I wish you

could hear and see it, but God is making it so that only I

can."

"No-no, it's fine. There's nothing to be sorry about."

"Just forget I said anything."

"No, this makes more sense to me now. I'd be honored to be your husband if that's what God wants me to do."

"You-you what? Slow down here. How can you accept this so easily?"

"Well, the suddenness and weirdness of it, the answer that's come to me through prayer, and the, uh, feeling that I have in my heart for you that I haven't felt with anyone else."

"Oooh, it's happening! I'm so happy for you! I knew God picked the right man."

"Hold on! I'm not rejecting you or anything. For some reason, I feel the same way about you, but can we slow down for a second and just be boyfriend and girlfriend before you marry me?"

"Yes, yes, of course! Sorry for making it seem like I'm already proposing to you."

"So, um, are we going to kiss?"

"You just said you wanted to slow down, but you want a kiss already?"

"Yeah, it's what a girl and boy do when they get into a relationship. What? Are you saying you don't want to kiss me?"

"No, no. It's just…umm…"

Before I know it, Connor grabs me and gives me a quick

kiss on the lips. I slap him in the face in response.

"Ow! What? What did I do

wrong?"

"You have to actually hold me and kiss me for a little longer. Come on! Do it right this time!"

"Alright, alright!" Connor does as I say and make the kiss last longer. At this moment, I feel the happiest I've ever felt in a while and complete in a way I can't explain. We smile awkwardly at each other before holding hands and continuing to walk down the

nature trail.

 You know what? I think I like

this new life that I've been given.

Chapter 3 - Struggling with the New

It's nighttime after a long day together. For the last few hours of the day, Connor and I ate dinner that I made and snuggled next to each other on the couch while watching TV. He gave me a kiss goodnight and said that he loves me and I said it back. Tomorrow, we're supposed to spend even more time with each other, but I can't wait that long, especially after what happened today, so I sneak into his room and lay down next to him.

Looking at his cute face and being this close to him is comforting and makes me feel so happy and at peace. His arms are at his side. What if I…Now I'm laying down on top of him. Ah! His arms are holding me now. Is he awake? Even while he's sleeping, he has that cute smile on his face that seems to be even happier now. Hmm. What if…I could take off his shirt. He might not like it, but I'm his girlfriend now and going to be his wife. There's nothing wrong with it. If he doesn't like it, I could strap him down and have my way with him and…

...

No, no, no. That'd be wrong to do. What am I thinking?

"Demons are tempting you again."

Could you get rid of them for me and get me out of this situation? I wouldn't want to hurt Connor or do something he'd hate me for.

"Already on it. I'll get Connor's arms off you."

When I get off Connor, the dirty thoughts go away. I then fall asleep and wake up later and see that Connor and I were holding one another and me having one of my legs over him.

"Good-good morning."

"Ah! What are you doing here?!" Connor says while jutting away from me as I still hold him.

"Calm down. I just want to, uhh, snuggle with you. There's nothing wrong with that now that we're in a relationship."

"There kind of is. It could invite temptations in your mind if you're not careful."

He's not wrong about that. "I'm sorry."

Connor kisses me and gets out

of bed. "It's okay. I'll make breakfast today."

"No, that's my job!" I say while

pulling Connor back down to the bed and heading to the

kitchen to make…

"Sausage and eggs."

Yes! That! After eating with Connor, we talk about what we should do today. Honestly, if had the bravery to say it, I'd tell him that I'd want to be near him all day, but after what happened this morning, I let him decide.

"How about you introduce me to your parents and I introduce you to mine?"

"Introducing you to my parents is a horrible idea. Why do we even have to do it anyway?"

"It's just a traditional thing to do. Besides, we're going to be married and seeing them a lot too."

"Well, I haven't talked to them in years since they kicked me out of the house."

"Why did they do that?"

"Because they wanted me to fend for myself when I turned eighteen. I had to find a job, a place to live, and go to college all by myself without anyone's help."

"That sucks, but they must've

thought you were-"

"They didn't think anything of me.

The only thing they cared about was going on vacations,

buying a thousand and one pieces of clothing, decorations

for the house, and having lots of money to spend. I would

typically be by myself in the care of a babysitter or one of their friends. In fact, I hardly spent any real time with them because of how much they loved to go out with each other while leaving me behind. Please, can we just forget about them like how they forgot about me?"

"They're still your parents and maybe they'll change when they see me and see how you're changing after what you've been through."

"Eh. I don't like it. I don't even have their number or know if there's a way to contact them."

"It should be simple with the internet. They also seem like the type of people to post everything they do on social media. What's their names and where do you remember them living?" After telling Connor what he wants to know, he looks on the internet for them and seems

to be concerned for a second. "Are these them?"

He hands me his phone with pictures of two people on it.

 "Yup. They look way older and

miserable in this picture than I remember, but this is

definitely them." I hand Connor back his phone. Now he

looks really concerned. "What is it?"

"…I'm sorry that there's no easy way to

say this, but they died a few years ago. Do you want to

know how?"

"Sure." Part of me is relieved that they're dead, and yet, a minor part is upset for some reason completely unknown to me.

"Their neighbors were wondering why they didn't see your parents for a while and assumed they were on another trip, but they eventually got curious and took a look inside to see your dad dead on the floor. The neighbors called the police so they could get the door open. They found your mom downstairs dead under some heavy boxes. Apparently, both died from heart disease, however, they didn't die quickly according to the medical examiner."

"I figured they would die like that one day. In fact, I hoped they would. They got what they deserved."

"How could you say that about your parents?"

"Because I hate them if I haven't made that clear enough."

"I found where they are buried. We should go see them."

"Why? It'd be a waste of time to visit those rotting pieces of crap."

"Again, they're your parents. You should pay them some respect. What could they possibly do to you now that they're dead?"

"Fine, let's go and get this over with since you're so adamant about it." Connor takes me on about a thirty-five-minute drive to where my parents are buried. When we find their gravestone, I can't help but feel that same split feeling of hatred and pity at the same time again.

Next to me, Connor silently prays. Is he praying for them? For what reason?

"Just in case their souls are in Purgatory, a place where repentant souls are purified before going to Heaven."

Pfft. If anything, they're probably in Hell. Do you know where their souls are?

"God has not allowed me access to that information."

What information do you have access to? Were the circumstances of their deaths a punishment for what they did?

"Yes, it was. It was also their last chance to repent, however, I don't know if they did."

They probably didn't. They never thought they were ever wrong. I spit on their graves and kick the gravestone over and over again. "Trash. See this, mom and dad? I'm going to be happier than you ever were. I hope it makes you jealous and your time in Hell worse."

"Gabriella, stop!"

"No! Let go of me! I have to make them pay!" Turning around, I try to slap Connor from stopping me from kicking my parent's grave. He stops my hand and slaps me in the face instead.

"Control yourself! Kicking their graves isn't going to make you happier or make them pay for what they've done to you."

"But it is making me happier! What should I be doing then?"

"This is going to sound weird and hard for you to do, but you should forgive them and let go of the grievances you have against them. It's the only way to get over them."

"I don't know if I could ever forgive them even if they came back to life and profusely apologized to me."

"That's why God brought me and you together. I'll help you move on from your anger."

Connor hugs and kisses me before asking me if I would like to go somewhere before we go out to dinner and I agree and randomly think of going to the nearby shopping outlet. It's where I used to go at least once every other week. To me, it was like going to a prize corner after work to cash in my paycheck to reward myself for all my work. Now, it reminds me of my parents always buying themselves things and how I'm so much like them than I'd like to admit. Because of that, I look around in the stores but don't get anything even when Connor offers to buy me something. Even so, he buys me some clothes so I don't have to keep wearing his.

After spending some time at the outlets, we go to a restaurant that's also a bar. While waiting to be seated, I catch a group of women looking at Connor, pointing at him, and presumably whispering about him, so I hold his arm, put my leg over his, and nest my head under his.

"Hm? Is something the matter, Gabriella?"

"Oh, it's nothing." Good. He's not noticing them at all, which means he only has eyes for me. I don't know why I think he wouldn't. Maybe I'm just being paranoid. We're called up to be seated and one of the women slaps Connor in the butt.

The woman who did it jokingly apologizes while giggling. I push Connor aside and get in the woman's face. "He's mine, hags. Piss off." If it wasn't for Connor pulling me back, I would've slammed the woman's head into the back of the wall and fought off her friends. Thankfully also, the women look scared of me and nothing else happens during and after we eat dinner.

 While sitting down watching TV back at home, I can't help but think about what happened today. "Hey, I'm sorry for trying to hit you and losing my temper today."

"It's okay. We'll work on that together. Tomorrow we'll go to church and then meet my parents for brunch."

"Do they already know we're coming over and our relationship?"

"Yup. I called and talked to them about it when I went to the bathroom during dinner."

It didn't occur to me that he was talking to his parents then. "I'm a little nervous about this, especially going to church since I never went there before. Maybe I should sit this Sunday out until I'm more religious like you are?"

"You have to start somewhere. Don't worry about it. Just do what I tell you and relax. No one is going to point out that it's your first time there."

"Um. Okay, I guess." For the rest of the night, I wait till Connor falls asleep first and he seems to be doing the same so he can go to bed, but I beat him by staying up the longest. I then quietly and carefully turn off the TV and put the blanket on both of us so we can snuggle together on the couch. To make sure that he doesn't sneak away from me, I put one of my legs over him and hold him in my arms. "I love you," I say before kissing him and falling asleep.

Chapter 4 – Seeing with the Soul

Huh? Where's Connor at?

Wasn't he here sleeping with me last night?

"He had to get up to get ready for church so I made sure you stayed asleep while he got up."

Aww. I wanted to cuddle more.

"Of course you would. You would've also made each other late for church. Speaking of which."

"Good to see you're awake, Gabriella. Get in your new clothes so we can head to church."

"Alright, alright." After getting changed, we go to church. It's a beautiful place with many pictures and statues. Everyone in it is dressed up in suits, dresses, and outfits that one would wear at an important event like a wedding. They seem to be quite at peace here.

Connor puts down the kneeler and prays silently like some of the people in here.

Not wanting to stick out, I do the same. Um. How do I do this? Hey!

"Sanctus, sanctus, sanctus!

Dominus deus sabaoth. Pleni sunt cæli et terra gloria tua.

Hosanna in excelsis."

He looks the happiest I've ever seen

him. What is he even saying? Everyone in the church says

the same thing during the mass. I've tried to follow

Connor's every move except for the part where they go up

to the altar for what they call communion. He doesn't want

me to go up for it and just stay kneeling for some reason. I

don't mind it, but I feel like I'm missing something

important. It's as if what they are receiving is calling to me

in some mysterious and silent way that only my soul can

hear.

 Even though I didn't receive what

they did, I feel a sense of peace by the end of it. At the

entrance of the church, Connor introduces me to the parish

priest who he's friends with, and tells him that we're going

to get married and that I haven't been baptized yet. The

priest is okay with this. In fact, he's glad that I'm getting in

touch with God. He then says he'll talk more with us about

arranging my baptism and our marriage later before saying goodbye to the other leaving churchgoers. To be honest, I thought being here would be a bit more awkward and boring, but I'm glad it wasn't.

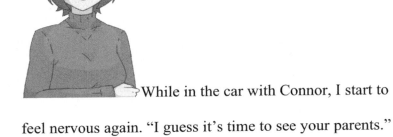

While in the car with Connor, I start to feel nervous again. "I guess it's time to see your parents."

"It's going to be okay. They get along with everyone! I wonder if my brothers and sisters are going to be there. Oh yeah, I forgot to mention that I had them. Do you have any siblings?"

"No, I don't." I have to be introduced to Connor's siblings too now? Oh, man. He tells me all about them and his parents on the way to his parent's house.

I try to be as calm as possible as we approach the door and ring the doorbell.

"Hello!" the man says before hugging Connor and me.

"Hey, dad. This is Gabriella."

"Hello, sir. It's an honor to meet you." I didn't even think about what I would say to his parents.

How do you introduce yourself as the woman your son is going to marry?

"The honor is mine. My name is William. Come in. My wife, Valentina, is almost finished making breakfast for us."

As we go in, I notice that Connor's parent's house is decorated like his with many religious statues and pictures along with pictures of his family. The woman in the kitchen must be his mother, Valentina.

Honestly, when looking at both of them, I'm not sure who Connor takes his looks after the most. "Hello, Gabriella. My name is Valentina. It's good to finally meet the woman that my son has been talking about a lot."

"It's good to meet you too."

"Take a seat and relax. Brunch is ready. Tell me all about yourself and how you met Connor. I want to know how you stole his heart so quickly."

"Tell you how

I…ummm…heh."

"Mom, you don't need to

cut to the chase so quickly."

"Oh, but I do. Her suddenly appearing in your life and you falling in love with her makes a mom like me overly curious as to how it all happened."

"I'll explain it while we eat."

After I say grace along with the family and we begin to eat, Connor explains how he met me, my circumstances, and what we've done since. Thankfully, he leaves out the time I tried to kill him and the two times I've tried cuddling with him.

"Wow, you've really been through a lot and changed a lot over the past few days, Gabriella. It really is an act of God."

"Yeah. I'm surprised you're not telling me to prove that I can see and have conversations with my guardian angel."

"It's fine. We believe you.

Now, for the big question. When are you two getting

married?"

"I still have to get the ring."

"Oh. Well, we have plenty of family rings you could use. Why don't you take one of those and propose to her right now? I want to record it and also have a framed picture of it."

"Um. I don't know. Hey, any of my brothers or sisters stopping by today?"

"No, but we should be seeing them soon for our monthly family dinner. We've made some changes to the house since you left. Want to see them while the girls continue their chatting?"

"Sure thing."

Oh no. Valentina is really forward with what she's thinking about. I'm not sure if I can sit here with her by myself. Where are they going anyway? They're not getting one of the rings, are they?

"Want to see Connor's baby photos? They're really cute."

"Okay." The photos that Valentina shows me are really cute. She describes each one as if they happened yesterday and says that seeing them makes her feel that way.

"How old are you?"

"Thirty-five." I stop myself before I ask her how old she is. She's probably older than me, but she looks younger.

"Connor is twenty-eight. Did you know that?"

"No, I didn't. My guardian angel did say he was young, but I didn't really think about how much younger or think to ask him his age."

"Don't worry. I don't have a problem with it. The age gap isn't too big and God did bring you two together."

"Right."

"How many kids are you planning on having?"

"Ummm. Uhhh." The thought of having children was in the back of my mind. Still, I never thought I'd have to answer how many I guess I should've because of Valentina's traditional mindset.

"You should aim for three or four. That's how many children I've had. Maybe I'll consider having a couple more in the future. I'm also fine with just one if that's all God chooses to give you."

"I ummm. Okay…" She really

is too much. I appreciate her bluntness, but still. Connor,

where are you?

"Since you've been living

together, have you also been sleeping with-"

"Hello, we're back! You weren't asking Gabriella any weird questions, were you, honey?" Thank God both of them are back!

"I was actually. I want to know if they slept togeth-"

"Come on, stop embarrassing them."

"Okay, fine. I still have more I want to talk about anyway."

"Actually, mom, we should go. We have a lot more things we wanted to do today, didn't we, Gabriella?"

"Yeah, let's go."

"You see? You've scared them off."

"Oops. I'm sorry. Come back soon!"

"Okay! Thanks for everything, mom and dad!" Connor says while taking my hand and quickly leaving the house. We get into the car, wave as we drive away, drive around the corner, and stop in a place where Connor's parents don't see us. "Whew! I hope mom didn't ask you anything too embarrassing."

"You heard what she was about to ask. Anyways, do we actually have any plans for the rest of the day?"

"I was thinking about going to the garden park by the lake for a bit and then I'll make dinner back home. It's Sunday so I thought we'd take it easy."

"I'd like that. Let's do it." Going to the garden park where many flowers and plants of the state are shown off in areas around the lake is a relaxing experience. Besides the gardens, there are small cafes, restaurants, and ice cream parlors here. There's also a playground, a small library, and a little carnival area with games for kids. It's great to see so many people happy in one area. What's also amazing and strange to me at the same time is that I see myself in the place of the mothers with their happy families as if I'm seeing a glimpse of my future self.

Connor and I don't talk much during our time here, but we don't need to since being with each other here is more than enough to keep me happy and worth it. We hang around until the fireworks show happens at sunset, kiss in front of it, and then go back home for dinner. Like the rest of the nights, we sit on the couch. This time we're watching some nostalgic movies.

Around ten o'clock, Connor says to me, "You know. I think I'll sleep with you on the couch tonight."

"A-are you sure?"

"Yeah. I don't really have work on Mondays. Sometimes I do and sometimes I have work on Saturdays depending on what parts of the diocese I have to help, but never mind it. Let's just rest together. We've had a long day."

"Yeah…"

This is the perfect way to end the day and I'll have Connor all to myself again for one more day. We cuddle up to one another and I fall asleep in Connor's arms. I get one more day with him. One more day...all to myself...

But his heart won't completely be mine. He's completely devoted to God, so he won't have me as the center of his world.

 That's fine. God is why Connor is such

a good person and it's better that he's this way so that he

can teach me to become better than I once was and happier

in life than my parents.

 But still, what happens if Connor

gets sick or is unable to work? I may not be able to get a

good job for a while because of my ruined reputation and

the remaining money in my bank account can only sustain

us for so long. My life is completely dependent on him.

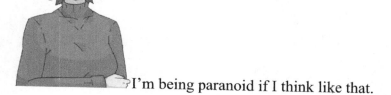

I'm being paranoid if I think like that.

Honestly, my life is better now than it was before. It's

strange to admit that I'm glad I lost everything I had and

got Connor in return. I'm sure he won't let me down and

we'll find a way to get through life's hardships together.

But what if God takes everything away

from me again? Who knows what he wants at any given

time? If I do what he wants, he'll chain me to his truth.

He'll chain my freedoms just like how my guardian angel

has chains.

I'll just have to trust Him then. He does seem to have my best interests in mind and has proved that I was on my way to ruin my life just like my parents ruined theirs.

I see that there's no changing your mind right now. I hope you enjoy giving your life to someone who took away everything you had.

Huh? I wasn't thinking to myself while asleep. Who was that?

"More demons trying to tempt you. I'm glad that you were able to prevent them from influencing you."

Why were they bothering me?

I've gone to church and prayed.

"That's exactly why they were after you. They leave those who are already chained to their sins alone."

 I'll also be chaining myself just

like that demon said if I pick God's side.

 "Such is life. You either chain

yourself to a loving or a hateful master. Who you chose

dictates how you live your life, values, goals, and

everything in between. There are no options besides these

two. I have chosen a loving master. What choice have you

made?"

I guess I've made the same choice you have seeing awful my life was with the other one.

"That makes me happier than you can possibly imagine. If the demons ever bother you again, I'll be here fighting for you. Do not be afraid to call on me whenever you need help."

I won't forget you, my guardian angel.

Epilogue – Broken Made New

When I wake up the next morning, I feel refreshed. Connor is up and making breakfast. We make plans to go out again this time going out to the beach. While walking around on the beach, I feel that something is off. Before I'm able to ask what's wrong, Connor gets on one knee in front of me and presents a gold, black, and red ring to me.

"Gabriella, will you marry me?"

"Yes, yes, I do!" Connor barely manages to get the ring on my finger before I tackle him and shower his face with kisses. Some of the people around us laugh.

"Okay, okay! Calm down. People are watching."

"So what? This is the happiest moment of my life. I'm going to enjoy it to its fullest."

"If you're going to do that, then I'll do the same," Connor says while reversing my hold on him, pinning me to the sand, and showering my face with kisses. As we look into each other's eyes, he says, "I love you."

"I love you too," I say before we kiss. For the next couple of hours, we sit on the beach enjoying the sights while holding each other's hands. We then get up around twelve and decide to get lunch on the boardwalk. "Um. Are we going to cuddle all night like we did last night?"

"I don't know. I have work and, knowing you, you'll try to keep me with you for as long as you want like you did this morning."

"And? What's your point? You can tell your boss that your crazy fiancée can't let go of you. I'm sure he'll understand."

"I don't think he'll accept me being late to work on a daily basis because of it." Connor's hand slips from mine because of his embarrassment, so I quickly grab it.

"Hey! I want to hold your hand for the entire day today. That means holding it while you're eating and driving too."

"Well, it can't be for the entire day. I'll eventually need to let go when I have to take a shower for tomorrow."

We could…no, no, no. At least not until we're married. "You still have to do what I want for the most part. You don't want to ruin this special day for me, do you? A happy wife means a happy life."

"I don't want to ruin it, but I don't have to do everything you want. It's my special day too."

"How about this? We wrestle over who gets to decide what we do for the rest of the day. Whoever gets the other to tap out wins, okay? Are you ready?"

"Wait, hold on!"

"Go!" I tackle Connor

again this time at a part of the beach where the water from

the ocean touches the beach so we end up getting wet. "Tap

out! You can't win."

"That's what you think!"

Connor and I wrestle together laughing and having a fun time until I end up tapping out. I don't mind that he gets to decide what we do today since I like most of the decisions he makes anyways. Without him, I'd be my old miserable self.

 Without what God did, I wouldn't be this happy, so I have to thank Him and my guardian angel as well. I thank you now and will continue to thank both of you until the day I die for all the blessings I have and will have in the future even if they come in the form of challenges and struggles because I know that there's something better at the end of it all.

The End

Behind the Story

- This story is inspired by *Romance Killer* by Wataru Momose and *My Divorced Crybaby Neighbor* by Zyugoya.

- Special thanks to Josh Contreras who introduced me to *Romance Killer*, the Netflix anime in particular, which was the main inspiration that got me started on this story.

- In the free eBook version of this story, Gabriella has a shotgun, but in this one, she has a pistol due to @An_dres_art changing it in his redraws. I don't know why he changed it. Speaking of his changes, because his emotes were a bit different than mine, I've had to change up the particular emote used in the story compared to the free version.

- There are also some corrections in this version that aren't in the free eBook version because the file size is too big for Smashwords all of a sudden.

The cover for the free eBook version of this story by @An_dres_art.

The original cover for this story that was made for the free eBook version created by Albert Oon.

The cover for this paperback version of this story by @An_dres_art.

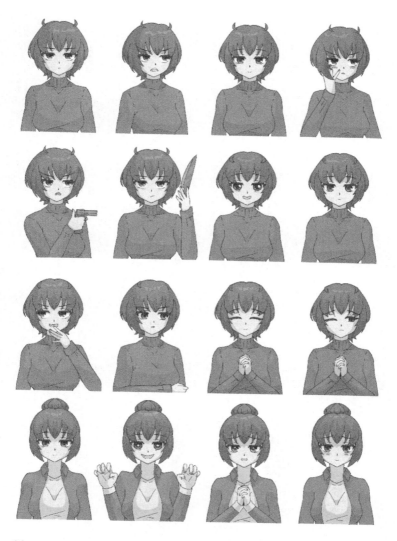

Character emotes remade by @An_dres_art.

The original character emotes for the free eBook version of this story made by Albert Oon.

All According to the Divine Plan: Author's Edition

If you liked this story, then check out these other ones!

There's a tradition that sacrifices their third child every generation for the continued prosperity and happiness of the family. Sakae is the next in her family to be sacrificed, but she won't let them take her life so easily even though she's trapped in a dimension that seems inescapable. She teams up with a boy she meets to find a way to escape and possibly stop this tradition of mass murder. This author's edition contains redone art, Behind the Story details, and concept art for those interested in seeing all the work done for this light novel-esque book.

War, Love, and the Absolute

Albert Oon

What does it mean to be yourself? There are those who are doctors, kings, queens, and heroes, and there are people who are simple farmers, caretakers, and soldiers. It takes some people lifetimes to find their role in life while some find it early in childhood. Through trials and tribulations, this series details the events that its characters go through to find themselves in this fairy tale and fantasy world. Even though they may become corrupted by conceit, mercy and a second chance are never too far away.

Cinis and Favilla are a couple trained to be the hope for the Kingdom of Fornax. Humanity fights against the forces of rot and decay with fire and light so that they can continue living, but these are uncertain times. "The greatest act of all is love," is the saying that Fornax goes by. Will the love between Cinis and Favilla be enough to hold them together through their challenges or will they eventually rot away like the rest of the world? Love burns brighter than fire in this fantasy tale with grand action scenes and moments to remember. This special edition of the story includes extra pictures and behind the scenes that details some of its influences.

This trilogy of supernatural thrillers has three stories in it with dozens of pictures and imagery to help bring the stories to life and for those who don't mind reading a non-traditional book. A family tradition that sacrifices the third child in the family for their continued happiness and prosperity, memories and strength won in a battle done in the flip of a coin, and a newlywed couple trapped in a dimension that tears apart bonds are just a few striking details of these stories.

Check out these free eBooks as well!

James and Julia secretly hate each other in their hearts and because of this, God forces them to inhabit the same body until they learn to love one another. The two are almost complete opposites. He makes friends, she keeps to herself. He doesn't try to help people, she makes it her career. He gives people the benefit of the doubt, she stereotypes them. Will they ever learn to love each other?

Peter's mother's dying wish is for him to be together with Rebecca, a lifelong friend. Since he fondly remembers being with her, he gives her a chance but is surprised when she tries to kill him. He hides in a house only to then be trapped in it with her. The house works against him while offering him and Rebecca the chance to live in their memories together forever while being able to change what happens and repeat them as many times as they wish.

In a beautiful crystal world, there is a world war between two kinds of dolls, the Flos and Crystallis. A mother and her son are caught in the conflict and the son is afflicted with a spell that will shatter him unless she gets to the springs, where all dolls came from. This mother will have to fight both nature and other dolls to help her son and do what a mother is supposed to for her child.

The land of Operetta is a demonic wasteland. The Church is keeping the threat within its borders to contain the threat. While they plan out how to help Operetta's people, two lovers are stuck in the middle of it all. They are separated from each other and can only communicate with one another through song. The two travel to meet each other. Will they survive the journey to reunite with each other?

Check out my blog, Albert Oon: Behind the Stories, for free short stories, free book samples, song/poem attempts, and more! Follow me on Twitter, Facebook, Instagram, and LinkedIn to see what I'm doing next.

Made in the USA
Middletown, DE
29 August 2023

37446345R00106